D0624906

POSTMAN PAT'S
TREASURE HUNT

WRITTEN BY
JOHN CUNLIFFE
ILLUSTRATED BY
CELIA BERRIDGE

FROM THE ORIGINAL TELEVISION DESIGNS BY IVOR WOOD

Postman Pat's Treasure Hunt first published in Great Britain
in 1981 by Andre Deutsch Limited
Text copyright © 1981 John Cunliffe
Illustrations copyright © 1981 Celia Berridge and Ivor Wood

Postman Pat's Secret first published in Great Britain
in 1982 by Andre Deutsch Limited
Text copyright © 1982 John Cunliffe
Illustrations copyright © 1982 Celia Berridge and Ivor Wood

Postman Pat's Difficult Day first published in Great Britain
in 1982 by Andre Deutsch Limited
Text copyright © 1982 John Cunliffe
Illustrations copyright © 1982 Celia Berridge and Ivor Wood

Postman Pat Takes a Message first published in Great Britain
in 1983 by Andre Deutsch Limited
Text copyright © 1983 John Cunliffe
Illustrations copyright © 1983 Celia Berridge and Ivor Wood

This edition first published in 1985 by
Octopus Books Limited
59 Grosvenor Street
London W1

ISBN 0 86273 177 1

Fourth impression, reprinted 1985

Produced by
Mandarin Publishers Limited
22a Westlands Road, Quarry Bay
Hong Kong

Printed in Hong Kong

Pat is the Greendale postman. Every day he drives his red van up the valley. Twisting along the twining roads; up and over the hills, far away; down narrow lanes and tracks to farms and cottages; by village, school and church; along by lakes and streams; he goes all over the valley. Everyone is glad to see him. He brings letters and cards; newspapers and magazines. He brings football-pools and catalogues and bills and birthday-cards and parcels full of who-knows-what? He also brings a smile, a joke, or a chat; news of the valley and who's-doing-what. He's cheerful and friendly and brightens every day. He has a little black cat, called Jess. Jess rides in a basket, next to Pat. Jess keeps an eye on things.

Each morning, Pat collects the day's post from the village post-office. Mrs. Goggins sorts the letters and parcels, ready for Pat to deliver, as well as looking after the shop. One sunny spring morning, Pat walked into the post-office with a,

"Good morning, Mrs. Goggins!"

"Good morning to you, Pat," said Mrs. Goggins, "and a busy one, too. Just look at all these letters and parcels!"

"And most of them for young Katy and Tom Pottage, it seems," said Pat.

"Well, of course, it's their birthday," said Mrs. Goggins, smiling.

"So it is," said Pat. "Mrs. Pottage was busy icing the cake yesterday. Aren't they lucky! How excited they'll be when they see all their cards and parcels. I'd better be on my way – they'll be looking out for me. Goodbye!"

"Goodbye Pat!"

Pat began the day's round. His first stop was at the village school. It was a very small school; there were only twelve children in it. Most of them came in a minibus that collected them from their farms and cottages. They arrived early – long before Mr. Pringle, their headmaster, drove up in his old Morris Minor. Pat arrived early, too. The children were playing in the yard. They came running up to Pat; each one had something to tell him and Pat usually had a joke to tell, or something to tease them with. Bill Thompson was the eldest and it was his job to look after the school's letters till Mr. Pringle arrived. This morning, someone gave him a push, and he dropped the letters, right in a puddle. The ink began to run. He wiped them on his shirt and made a lovely inky pattern all down his front. Sarah Gilbertson was showing Pat a fossil, so he didn't notice. Then Sarah and Lucy Selby asked Pat if he was good at hopscotch, as they had just had new lines painted in the yard.

"Well, it's a long time since I played," said Pat, doubtfully. He had a try, anyway, and he was quite good at it, but it made his postman's hat joggle up and down. He was enjoying the hopscotch so much, that he almost forgot the time.

"Good gracious!" he said, looking at his watch, "I'll have to be off. The post mustn't be late, not to-day, of all days."

"What's special about to-day?" asked Sarah.

"Wait and see," said Pat. "Cheerio! I'll see you to-morrow."

A little further along the road, Pat turned in at the gates of Greendale Farm. As soon as they heard Pat's van, Katy and Tom Pottage came running out to meet him. When they saw the pile of letters and parcels in Pat's arms, all for them, they couldn't wait to open them. As they are twins, it was a *double* birthday.

Mrs. Pottage came out with a pair of scissors and they sat down on the grass, and snipped their parcels open. They had some lovely presents, but Katy did not seemed pleased with hers.

"What's up with Katy?" said Pat.

"She's wrong side out to-day," said Mrs. Pottage. "She's lost Sarah-Ann."

"Is that the little doll she takes to school?"

"She takes it *everywhere*," said Mrs. Pottage. "She's lost without it; I don't know what we'll do if it doesn't turn up."

"It's sure to turn up somewhere," said Pat.

"The trouble is, it could be almost anywhere," said Mrs. Pottage. "We went to see Aunt Alice yesterday and called at ever so many places on the way. She could have left it just anywhere."

"I'll look out for it," said Pat. "You never know, I might spot Sarah-Ann in my travels. I'm good at finding things. Poor Katy – she *does* look sad. I'll do my best. Don't worry now! Cheerio."

Pat was on his way again, in his red van. He told Jess about the lost doll. Where *could* Sarah-Ann be? Jess looked thoughtful and kept a sharp lookout for any wandering dolls as they travelled from farm to farm. He could catch mice in the dark, so surely he could catch a doll in broad daylight.

The next stop was the church. The Reverend Timms had heard Pat's van coming, and was looking out to see if there were any letters to-day. There was a card for him, from his Aunt Joan, on holiday in Majorca. Pat told him about Katy's lost doll.

"She could have left it in church," said the Reverend Timms. "She always brings it. 'Seek and thou shalt find.' Let's have a look. Mind your head."

They searched among the pews, looking under the seats, lifting hassocks, moving piles of hymn-books, creeping about and popping up in unexpected places. There were so many places to look in, in a church. At last, the Reverend Timms *did* find something, but it was not Sarah-Ann. It was a lady's glove.

"Let me see, I think I know that glove," said Pat. "Look, it has letters sewn inside. 'D.T.' Dorothy Thompson – that's whose it must be. I'll take it along for her; she *will* be pleased."

"Well, I hope Katy's doll does turn up," said the Reverend Timms.

"'Let the Lord guide you, and all will be well.'"

"Yes, we'll keep looking till we find it," said Pat. "Thanks for helping! Goodbye!"

Pat drove up the steep hill to Thompson Ground. Mrs. Thompson *was* surprised when Pat gave her a glove with her letters.

"Well I never," she said. "Where did you find my glove? I've been looking everywhere for it."

Then Pat told her about Katy's doll being lost. "We were looking in the church for it, and the Reverend found your glove instead."

"Well, Katy and her mum did call in for a cup of tea, on Monday – she could have left her doll here; perhaps it's under a cushion – we'd better have a look."

They searched everywhere. They lifted cushions; they looked under chairs and behind chairs; they peered behind the television-set and amongst the coats that hung on the back of the door; they even moved the sideboard out from the wall, to see if Sarah-Ann had slipped down the back. It was no good; they didn't find Katy's doll; but Mrs. Thompson found a knife down the side of a chair.

"That's Ted Glen's knife," said Pat. "It's his rabbiting knife."

"Goodness knows when he left it here, he hasn't been here since last Christmas," said Mrs. Thompson.

"I'll take it along for him," said Pat; "he will be pleased to have it back."

"I hope you find Katy's doll," said Mrs. Thompson.

"We'll keep looking. See you to-morrow! Cheerio!"

"Cheerio, Pat!"

Pat drove down the steep and winding road, and along the valley to Ted Glen's cottage. Jess kept a sharp lookout for the lost doll.

"What a day!" said Pat. "We've found a glove *and* a knife, but no Sarah-Ann. I wonder if we will find her – I *do* hope so."
Jess twitched his whiskers hopefully.

Ted Glen was delighted to see his knife. He couldn't guess where Pat had found it. Pat told him about Katy's lost doll. Ted said –

"They popped in, yesterday, with a lamp they wanted mending. She could have left the doll here."

So they went to have a look in Ted's workshop. What a jumble it was. There were things everywhere; all the things that people had brought to be mended. There were toys and television-sets; cookers and cake-stands; bikes and roller-skates; farm-machines and house-machines, more than you could count. Goodness knows when Ted would mend them all! Likely enough, most of them had been quite forgotten by their owners. And what a dreadful place it was in which to seek a doll. There were so many things that they could hardly move: they lifted things, they fell over things, things fell on them, they moved things, they pushed things, they looked over things,

they looked round things, under things, behind things, between things, beside things. They did not find Sarah-Ann, but Ted found a watch that he'd mended then forgotten about.

"That's Miss Hubbard's," he said. "She brought it to be fettled, last Christmas. Could you take it along for her, Pat? She'll be needing it."

"Certainly, I'm going that way."

"I hope you find the doll," said Ted.

"So do I," said Pat. "I seem to be able to find plenty of other things."

Pat drove along the valley to Southlands Farm Cottage where Miss Hubbard lives. The mobile-shop was already there and Miss Hubbard was doing her shopping, filling her basket with groceries. She was pleased to see Pat and even more pleased when he handed her a watch with her letters, though she couldn't guess where Pat had found it. Sam came to see what they were talking about and to add up Miss Hubbard's shopping. (Sam drives the mobile-shop.) So Pat told them both about Katy's lost doll, but they hadn't seen it.

"Poor Katy," said Pat, "and on her birthday, too. I'll buy her a box of chocolates to cheer her up, as we haven't found Sarah-Ann." Pat took a box of chocolates from the shelf of the mobile-shop. There was something else on the shelf; a squashed-up something that had been behind the box of chocolates.

"What's that," said Pat, "behind your chocolates?"

"I don't know," said Sam. "It's nothing I put there." Pat pulled the bundle out, and straightened it and smoothed it.

"I know what it is," he said.

"It's a doll," said Miss Hubbard.

"I don't sell dolls," said Sam.

"It isn't a new one," said Miss Hubbard.

"It's Katy's doll," said Pat. "There's her name, sewn in the skirt. It must be Sarah-Ann; the one we've been looking for all day!"

Sam was amazed.

"That young Katy Pottage," he said. "She gets everywhere."

"I'll take the chocolates, anyway," said Pat. "They'll make a nice birthday present."

Jess guarded Sarah-Ann all the way back to Katy's farm; he wasn't going to let her slip away again. And when Pat arrived at the twins' birthday-party, with Sarah-Ann *and* the chocolates, Katy smiled properly for the first time that day. She hugged Sarah-Ann and Pat and Jess, and said "Thank you" to them all. Pat just had to join in the party and Jess sat beside him. There was tea and cakes for Pat and a saucer of cream for Jess.

It was a good party.

Then Pat looked at his watch, and said, "Time we were going. Goodbye everyone! Have a good time!"

"Goodbye Pat! Goodbye!" everyone called and off went Pat and Jess in their red van.

Pat still had to collect the letters from the letterbox and tell Mrs. Goggins all about his treasure hunt for Katy's lost doll.

POSTMAN PAT'S SECRET

WRITTEN BY
JOHN CUNLIFFE

ILLUSTRATED BY
CELIA BERRIDGE

FROM THE ORIGINAL TELEVISION DESIGNS BY IVOR WOOD

It was a special day for Pat. He wouldn't tell anyone why it was a special day, because it was his secret, a secret that he had kept for many years. Pat sang as he drove along the valley; it was a happy day, too. Jess sat beside him, and twitched his whiskers.

"Now, young Jess, don't you give my secret away," said Pat. Jess promised not to say one word about it.

When Pat arrived at the village post-office, Mrs. Goggins was looking out for him and she was looking very pleased about something.

"Hello, Pat," she said, "there's such a lot of post to-day!"

Pat didn't look too pleased, until he saw that much of it was for him. But who could be writing all these letters to Pat? One had a drawing of a cat on it, and the writing looked suspiciously like Katy Pottage's.

"Why don't you open them?" said Mrs. Goggins, "Then you'll know who sent them."

So Pat did.

What a surprise! They were all birthday-cards.

He stood them in a row along the counter. There was one from every person on his round. He was very pleased, after all, but how did everyone know that it was his birthday to-day? *That* was his secret, and now it was no longer a secret at all.

"How did they know?" said Mrs. Goggins. "Well, *I* didn't tell them and that's all I'm saying, except – Happy Birthday, Pat, and many happy returns."

Pat bought six chocolate kittens, then gathered up all his cards, and the day's letters, and went on his way.

At Greendale Farm, the twins were looking out for Pat, and sang "Happy Birthday To You", when he came in with the letters, and Mrs. Pottage joined in, too.

Pat showed them all his cards. Then Mrs. Pottage whisked a cloth off the table, and there was a birthday-cake, with an icing-sugar post-office van on it, and pink letters saying BIRTHDAY GREETINGS TO POSTMAN PAT. And there was a sugar-mouse for Jess.

"But how did you know it was my birthday?" said Pat.

"We're not telling," said Mrs. Pottage. "It's a secret."

"It *was* a secret," sighed Pat. "But, all the same. . .thank you very much; it is a lovely cake."

Then he was off on his way.

"Goodbye!"

The church was the next stop, as there were some letters for the Reverend Timms.

"And here's something for you, on your birthday," said the Reverend. He gave Pat a Bible, bound in leather.

"That's very kind of you," said Pat, "but how did you know it was my birthday?"

"He who reads shall learn," said the Reverend Timms.

"Oh?" said Pat, puzzled. How could the Bible tell the secret of his birthday? He couldn't guess.

When Jess saw it, he wondered if it was a sugar-bible.

Pat drove away, up the winding hilly roads, and arrived at Thompson Ground just in time for a cup of tea. Mrs. Thompson was just looking at Pat's birthday-cards, when Alf came in.

"Hello, Pat," he said, "and a very happy birthday!"
He gave Pat a walking-stick, with a curly horn handle, that he'd made himself.
"That'll be good for keeping dogs off," he said.
"Thank you," said Pat, "it will be very useful, but *how* did you know it was my birthday?"
"Oh, you'll find out for yourself. Just keep your eyes open," said Alf, smiling. "You're quite a famous postman, you know."

"Whatever does he mean?" thought Pat, as he waved goodbye to the Thompsons. He was getting more and more puzzled, and his van was filling up with presents. Jess didn't like the sheep's horn on the walking-stick; he thought it might butt him when he wasn't looking.

When Pat called on Granny Dryden, she gave him a woolly vest that she had knitted specially. It looked *very* itchy!

And Miss Hubbard gave him a steering-wheel cover, made of red velvet, to keep his hands warm in winter.

At Intake Farm, George Lancaster gave Pat two dozen eggs, all different colours, laid by his prize hens.

When Pat met Sam Waldron, along the road, with his mobile-shop, Sam gave him a big box of strawberries, and carton of cream.

Pat called late at the village school because they'd all been away for the morning, on a visit to Pencaster Castle. They were ready for Pat, though, all the same. They sang him two songs that they had been practising, and gave him a big model of his van that they had made specially.

Pat had presents for them – a chocolate kitten each – to say thank you for all their cards. How pleased they were! But when he asked how they knew about his birthday, the children smiled, pressed fingers to their lips and said nothing.

Pat must get on his way home now. He did not want to be late, because he knew his wife would have a special birthday meal ready for him. The day's round was finished, and Pat's last job was to empty the letter-box.

Peter Fogg came along on his tractor, and stopped for a chat. Pat told him about how everyone knew his birthday.

"Don't you know why?" said Peter, laughing.

"I certainly do *not*!" said Pat.

Peter pulled a newspaper out of his pocket. It was the Pencaster Gazette.

"Have a look at this," he said.

Pat was amazed. There was a piece all about him, headed POSTMAN OF THE YEAR. It told the story of his work, and how he helped everyone he met, where he had been to school, where he was born, and *when* he was born!

"*Well*," said Pat, "so that's how everyone knew. I'll be *bothered*, these newspaper people, they find everything out." He was cross and pleased, at the same time.

"Keep it as a souvenir," said Peter.

"Thanks," said Pat, "and that surely is my last present to-day."

"What next?" thought Jess. "We'll never get home at this rate."

But they were on their way home this time.

"I wonder when *my* birthday is?" said Jess to himself. "It's such a good secret that even *I* don't know! I wish I could find it in the paper, then *I* could have cards and presents. Never mind, there'll be a good dinner waiting for me, and that's as good as a birthday any time."

"What a strange day," said Pat. "We've finished up with a van full of letters and parcels."

And off they went home; but Jess didn't have his usual cat-nap – he wanted to keep an eye on that ram's horn, just in case it tried anything funny.

POSTMAN PAT'S
DIFFICULT DAY

WRITTEN BY
JOHN CUNLIFFE

ILLUSTRATED BY
CELIA BERRIDGE

FROM THE ORIGINAL TELEVISION DESIGNS BY IVOR WOOD

It was a lovely morning in Greendale. The sun was shining. The birds were singing. Where was Postman Pat? It was long past his time to be up and on his way, but his curtains were closed and his van stood outside. All was silent and still. Then . . . the door opened and Pat looked out. He looked sleepily at his watch. "Oh dear, is it *that* time?"

He dressed and rushed out without any breakfast, and without his hat! He dashed back for his hat, fell over his cat, and landed in a heap on the doorstep.

He picked Jess up and ran to his van, saying, "Come on, let's get moving, Jess. We're ever so late."

He talked to Jess as they drove along the winding roads.

"What a start to the day! I wonder why that blooming alarm-clock didn't go off? We'll have to see if Ted can mend it."

Mrs. Goggins was having a difficult morning, too. She was trying to mend a parcel. It was for Ted Glen. When Pat arrived he tried to help, but they got all tangled up in sticky tape! What a muddle!

"I do wish people would wrap parcels up properly," said Mrs. Goggins. "This is in a right old mess – and heavy, too. I don't know what Ted will say."

"It's just one of those days," said Pat. "First I slept in, because my alarm didn't go off, then this parcel. Never mind, it's a lovely morning. Cheerio!"

Pat was on his way. He saw Ted, mending a fence on the hillside.
   "Hello," he said, "there's Ted. I'll give him his parcel before it falls to bits."
He stopped and shouted to Ted, "Hi! Ted – there's a parcel for you."

Ted came down the hill. Pat passed the parcel to him over the wall. He was just saying, "Be careful, Ted, it's a bit loose," when. . . . "Ooooooooops!" it slipped, and Ted dropped it.

"Oh *no!*"

Dozens of little balls, and wheels, and screws, rolled away into the grass. Ted, on his hands and knees, began to scratch and search for them.

"Nay," he said, "I'll never find them in all this long grass."
"Hold on," said Pat, climbing over the wall, "I'll give you a hand."
"It's hopeless," said Ted.

When Bill Thompson saw them, he came over to see what they were doing.

"I have just the thing," he said. It was a large magnet. It picked up all the wheels, and balls, and screws from the grass.

"I hope they're all there," said Pat.
"I'll count them," said Ted. "Thanks."
"Cheerio Ted."
"Cheerio Pat."
Ted said, "Thanks," to Bill; "That was real handy."

Pat's next stop was at Thompson Ground. Alf was up a ladder, mending the barn wall. Pat was just walking under the ladder, when Alf shouted, "Look out!"
Too late!

"Oooooooohhhhh! Ouch!" said Pat.

Alf had dropped his tin of nails. Pat tried to catch it – twisted round – lost his balance – and sat down with a bump, with his hand twisted under him. Alf came down the ladder.

"You all right, Pat?"

"No, I think I've sprained my wrist."

"I'll go and get a bandage," said Alf.

Then Mrs. Thompson came along.

"Dear me, whatever have you been up to, Pat?"

"Just in too much of a hurry," said Pat. "Walking under ladders."

Mrs. Thompson looked at his wrist. "Now hold still," she said, "and I'll bind it up for you. But you won't be able to drive any more to-day, you know. You'll have to rest it."

"What about all my letters?" said Pat.

Sam Waldron arrived in his mobile-shop. They told him about Pat's accident.

"Why don't you put your letters and parcels in my van?" said Sam. "We can do our rounds together."

"And the post will get through after all," said Pat. "Thanks, Sam; it's a grand idea."

Everyone helped to move the parcels and letters into Sam's van.

"There's plenty of room," said Sam." Just stack them at the back of the van behind the seats."

"Come on, Jess," said Mrs. Thompson. She put Jess on the seat. "You'll be all right in there."

Pat climbed in beside Sam, and Jess curled up on his knee.

"Off we go," said Sam.

Away they went.
  "What a surprise everyone will get, when they see us together," said Pat.
And so they did.

Pat's hand was still hurting, so they made their first stop at Dr. Gilbertson's house. She had a good look at his hand, and said, "It's not broken. You'll be all right in a day or two. I'll just give you something to soothe it."

She gave him a jar of cream that took the pain away.

"Thank you, doctor," said Pat. "Cheerio!"

On they went to Greendale Farm.

"What a good idea," said Mrs. Pottage, when she saw them. "We can get our post and parcels with our potatoes and peas."

All the people of Greendale agreed with her, as Pat and Sam went on their way. The Reverend Timms ... Miss Hubbard ... Granny Dryden ... George Lancaster ... Peter Fogg ... and all the children.

Jess liked Sam's van, too, because the smell of fish tickled his nose. At the end of the day, Sam gave Jess a kipper all to himself, and that turned a difficult day into a perfect day, as far as Jess was concerned.

POSTMAN PAT
TAKES A MESSAGE

WRITTEN BY
JOHN CUNLIFFE

ILLUSTRATED BY
CELIA BERRIDGE

FROM THE ORIGINAL TELEVISION DESIGNS BY IVOR WOOD

The wind had been blowing and banging all night in Greendale. When morning came, Postman Pat set out on his round. He drove his red van and his cat, Jess, sat by his side. What a mess the wind had made!

All along the valley, branches had been blown off the trees. Many were scattered on the roads and Pat had to dodge the big ones as he drove along. By Greendale Farm, a whole tree had blown down, just missing Peter Fogg's cottage. Some telephone-wires were broken too.

"Dear me," said Pat, "that's a nuisance. There'll be a fair number of telephones out of action, now."

Then, as they came to the vicarage, he stopped.

"I wonder if the Reverend kept that stamp for me? Better pop in and see him
. . . I hope he remembered."

The Reverend Timms was busy. He seemed to be packing his cases to go on
holiday.

"Hello, Reverend!" called Pat. "I just popped in to see if you kept that Australian stamp for me, yesterday."

"Of course, Pat," said the Reverend Timms, "just the thing for your collection . . ."

"Thanks," said Pat, "but where are you off to?"

"I'm off to London! To meet my sister, Elsie . . . that's what the letter was all about . . . she's flying over from Australia . . . haven't seen her for years . . . what a rush! Now, *where* did I put that stamp? Ah, *here* it is."

"Thank you," said Pat.

The Reverend picked the telephone up to see if it was working. No luck! "Such a nuisance," he said. "The phone's not working, so I'll have to rush round and see everyone, to cancel the church meetings while I'm away. Such a bother, with a train to catch ..."

"It's this wind," said Pat. "It's brought the wires down."

"Well, I'll just have to hurry. The train goes at ten o'clock."

"I hope you get round in time," said Pat. "Cheerio! Have a good trip! Thanks for the stamp!"

Pat was on his way.

He called at the post-office for the letters.
"Morning, Mrs. Goggins! I'm not late, am I?"

"Not really," said Mrs. Goggins, "but I thought you might have trouble getting through, what with all these trees being blown down."

Pat told Mrs. Goggins about the Reverend Timms' letter, and his trip to London, and his telephone being out of order.

"Ee it's a bad job, isn't it," she said. Then her telephone began to ring.

"*My* phone's working, anyway. Hello – Greendale post-office here – who is it? Elsie Timms? Urgent message for the Reverend Timms? Yes . . . his phone *is* out of order . . . yes . . . your flight diverted to Manchester?"

"Oh dear," said Pat.

"You'll come on to Greendale by car? Yes . . . I'll ask our postman to dash over and tell the Reverend not to go to London after all – he might just catch him."

"I've got the message," said Pat. "Tell her I'm on my way."
"Bye, Pat! I hope you're on time. Bye!"
Pat dashed out to his van.
"Hold tight, Jess; it's full speed ahead."

Along the twisting roads they went, back to the vicarage. Pat knocked on the door, but the vicar had gone.

"I'll leave a note for him," said Pat, "in case he calls back before he catches his train. Let's see, he's sure to call on Miss Hubbard. We'll try and catch up with him there. Come on, Jess, we can take a short cut along the back road."

Pat jolted off along the bumpy back road to Miss Hubbard's. It was a very rough ride. And then, when they were almost there, the road was blocked by Peter Fogg's trailer. There wasn't even enough room to turn round and go back. So Pat jumped out, put Jess in his bag, and ran across the field to Miss Hubbard's cottage.

"Hello, Pat," said Miss Hubbard, "what's all the hurry, and where is your van?"

"Morning, Miss Hubbard," Pat panted, "I'm trying to catch up with the Reverend Timms. Have you seen him?"

"Oh, he went a few minutes ago. He's in a hurry too; he wants to catch a train."

"I must catch him before he does," said Pat. "I have an urgent message for him."

"He did say he was calling on Ted Glen. You might catch him there. Quick! You can borrow my bike. Go on!"

Pat put Jess in the basket, and wobbled away, gathering speed. He called over his shoulder –

"Thanks, Miss Hubbard! I'll try anything ... hold tight, Jess!"

Pat whizzed, and jolted, and wobbled his way to Ted Glen's; but he couldn't stop when he arrived, and he crashed into the workshop-door, and tumbled in a heap on the floor.

"Hello, Pat, whatever are you doing?" said Ted. "Are you all right?"

"Yes, I think so. I'm trying to catch up with the Reverend."

"You're too late," said Ted. "The Reverend's gone; but he said he would call on Granny Dryden, before he catches his train." But when Pat tried the bike, the front wheel wouldn't go round.

"Leave it to me," said Ted. "I'll fettle it. You can borrow these roller-skates. I've just mended them. You'll fairly move when you get these on."

"Well, I said I'd try anything," said Pat, "and we must catch the Reverend before he catches his train. Thanks, Ted. Here we go again ... Ooooooooooops!"

Pat shot out of Ted's workshop like a rocket, and away along the road to Granny Dryden's. *But*, he had forgotten to ask Ted where the brakes were! When he came to a sharp bend in the road, he was going too fast to get round the bend, and too fast to stop. So he did a somersault over the gate and landed in a soft patch of mud.

Sam Waldron's van was coming along the road. The Reverend Timms was riding in it, as Sam was giving him a lift to the station.

"I thought I saw Pat dive over that gate," said Sam. He stopped his van to get a better look.

Then, Pat scrambled to his feet and waved to them.

"It *is* Pat," said Sam.

"Hello, Sam! . . . and Reverend!" called Pat. "I've caught you at last. Thank goodness you've not gone to London."

Pat told the Reverend all about his sister's phone message, and how he must not go to London after all, as she was coming straight to Greendale.

"Lord bless us," he said, "what a good thing you caught me in time. I'd have gone traipsing off to London and missed Elsie, and she would have been here looking for me! After all that rush, too! Never mind, all's well in the end. Thank you so much, Pat. Let's go home, Sam, and we'll have a nice cup of tea. Can we give you lift, Pat?"

But Peter Fogg came along, with his tractor and trailer. When he heard the story, he said,

"It's my fault that Pat had to leave his van. I left my trailer in the road. I'll give you a lift back to your van, Pat."

"And I'd better get along to meet my sister," said the Reverend Timms. "God speed! And thanks to all!"

So Pat and Jess rode back on the trailer. Pat was glad to see his van again. As for Jess, he never wanted to see a bike or a roller-skate again. He curled up thankfully on his seat, as Pat drove on his way. As they passed the vicarage, the Reverend was just carrying a suitcase in, with an Australian label on it.

"She's arrived," he said. "I was back just in time, thanks to you, Pat. And I found your pen on my doorstep."

"Thanks," said Pat. "I hope your sister enjoys her visit. Cheerio!"

"Thanks, Pat. Bye! Bye, Jess!"

"Now we'll get the letters delivered," said Pat to Jess. "That bothersome wind – it's made a real mischief of itself, to-day."